# TO MAD BEAR, WHO IS ALWAYS TEACHING ME HOW TO COLOR OUTSIDE THE LINE.

Text and illustrations © 2022 Thao Lam

Owlkids Books acknowledges the financial support of the Canada Council for the Arts, the Ontario Arts Council, the Government of Canada through the Canada Book Fund (CBF) and the Government of Ontario through the Ontario Creates Book Initiative for our publishing activities.

Published in Canada by Owlkids Books Inc.,
1 Eglinton Avenue East, Toronto, ON M4P 3A1

Published in the US by Owlkids Books Inc.,
1700 Fourth Street, Berkeley, CA 94710

Library of Congress Control Number: 2021951886

Library and Archives Canada Cataloguing in Publication

Title: The line in the sand / [written and illustrated] by Thao Lam.
Names: Lam, Thao, author, illustrator.
Identifiers: Canadiana 20210389702 | ISBN 9781771475709 (hardcover)
Classification: LCC PS8623.A466 L56 2022 | DDC jC813/.6—dc23

Edited by Karen Boersma | Designed by Alisa Baldwin

Manufactured in Guangdong Province, Dongguan City, China, in March 2022, by Toppan Leefung Packaging & Printing (Dongguan) Co., Ltd.
Job #BAYDC103

A     B     C     D     E     F

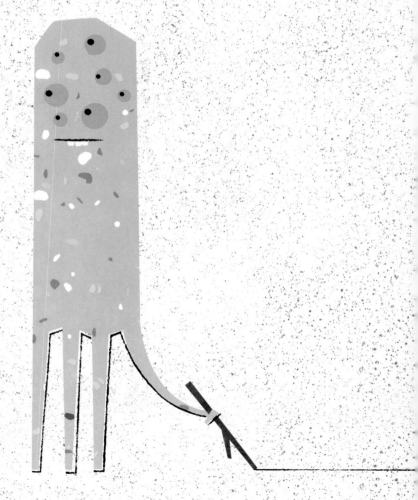

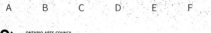  

ONTARIO ARTS COUNCIL
CONSEIL DES ARTS DE L'ONTARIO
an Ontario government agency
un organisme du gouvernement de l'Ontario

Canada Council for the Arts     Conseil des Arts du Canada

Canada

FSC
MIX
Paper from responsible sources
FSC® C104723

  Publisher of Chirp, Chickadee and OWL
www.owlkidsbooks.com

Owlkids Books is a division of  bayard canada

THAO LAM

# THE LINE IN THE SAND

OWLKIDS BOOKS

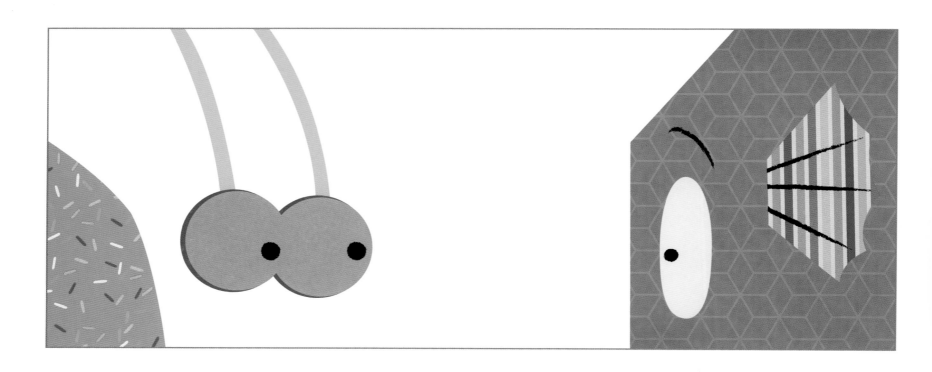

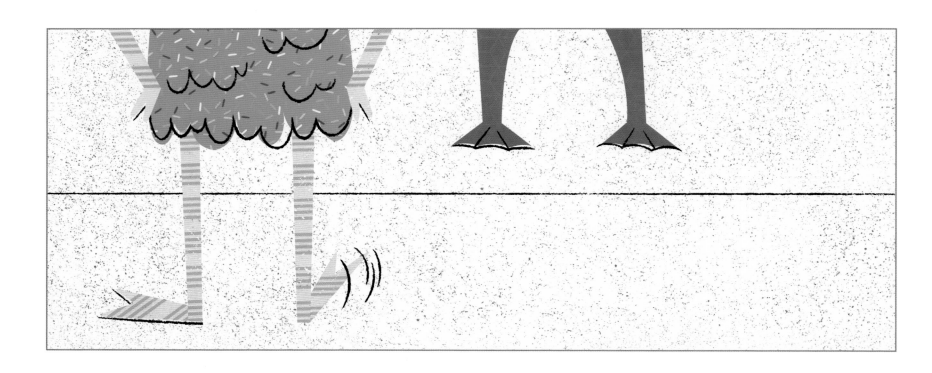

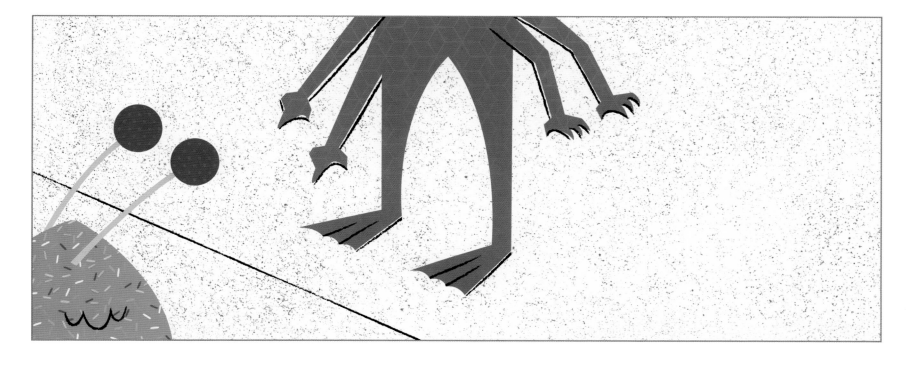

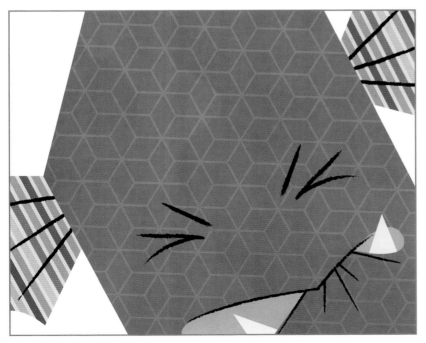

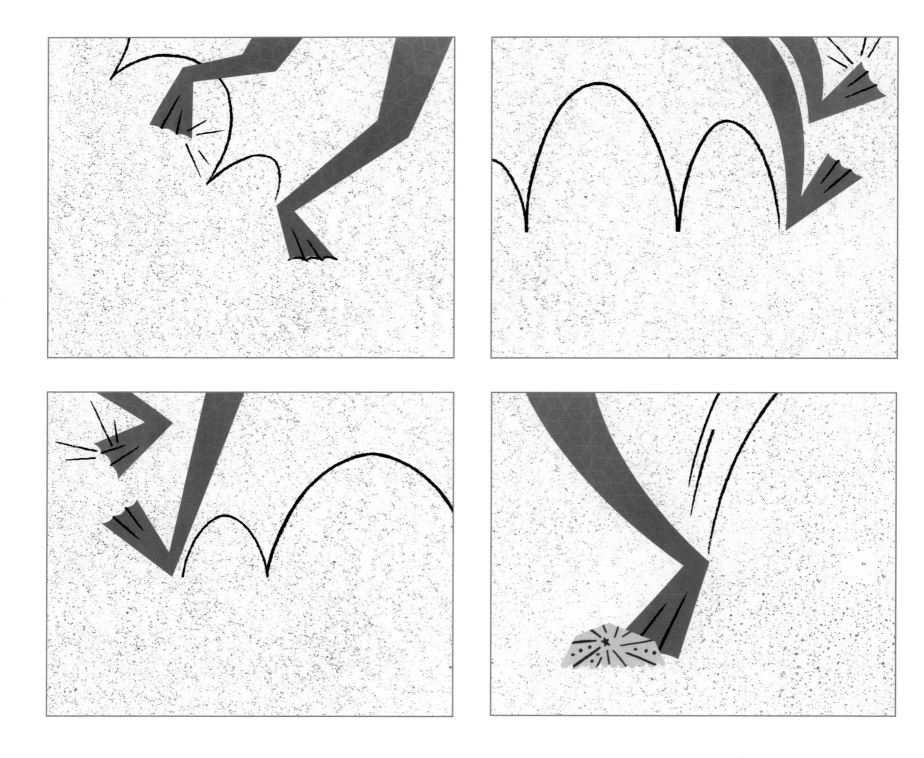

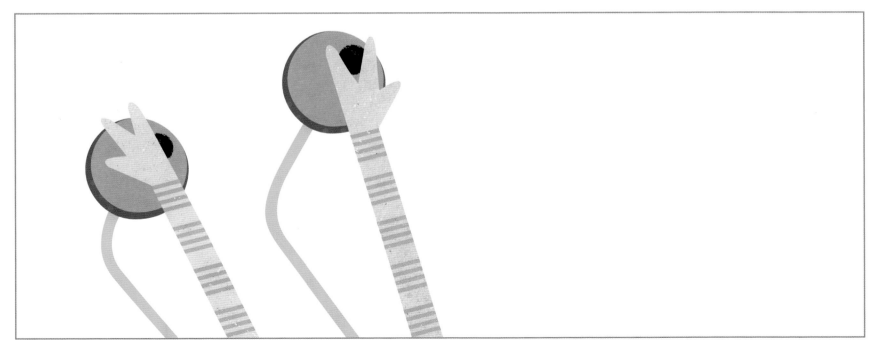

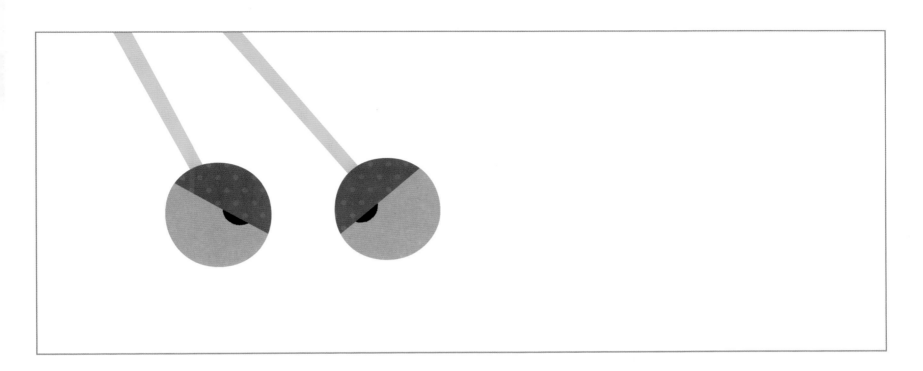

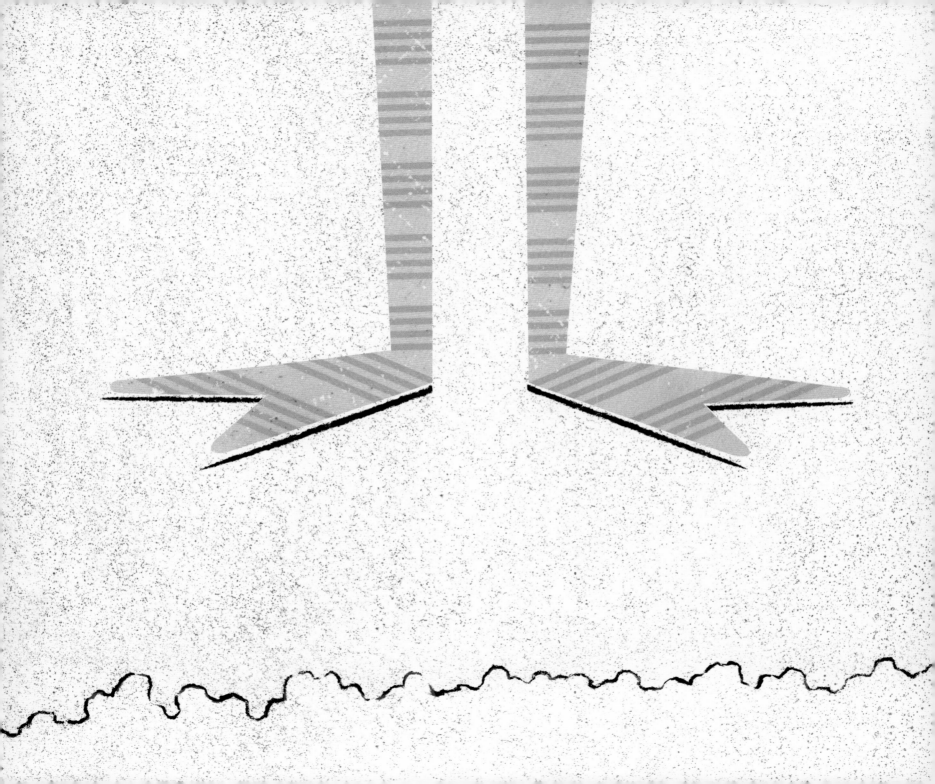

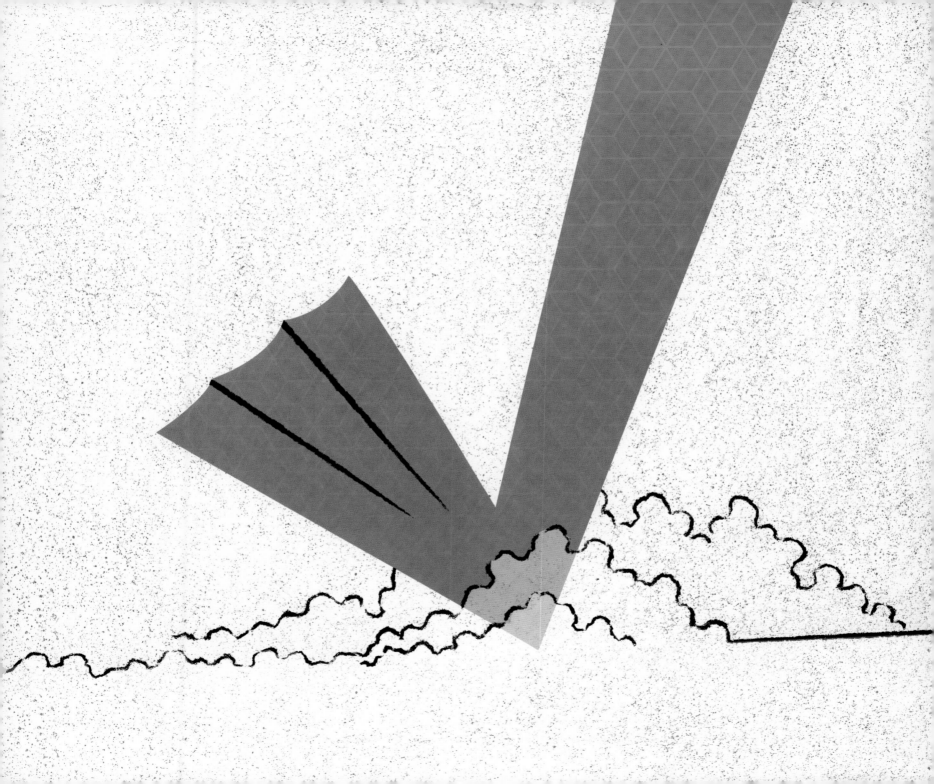

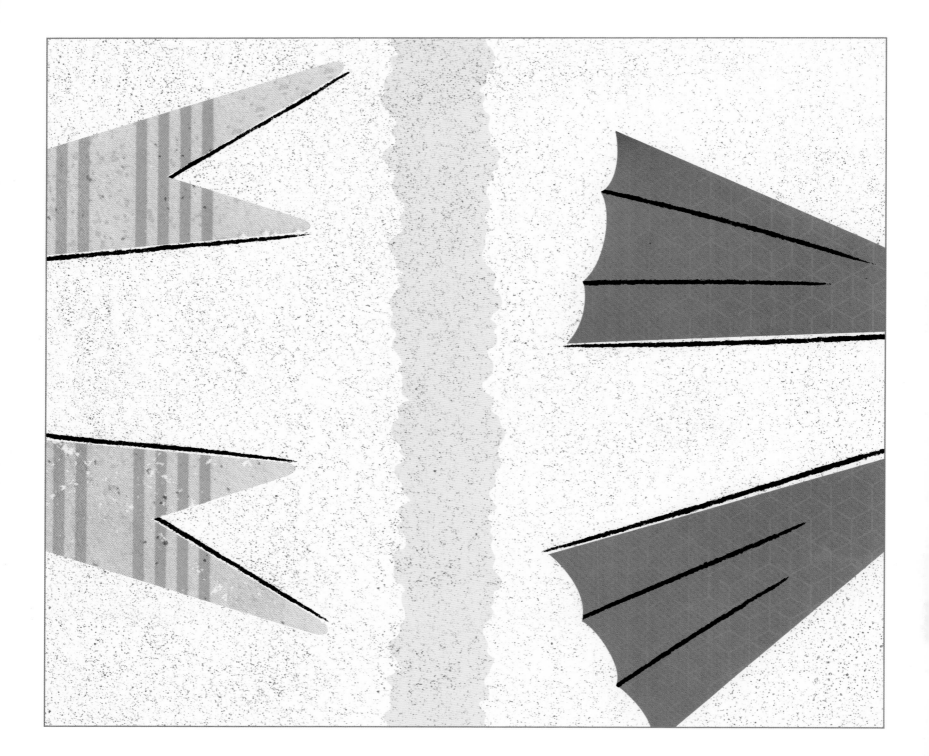

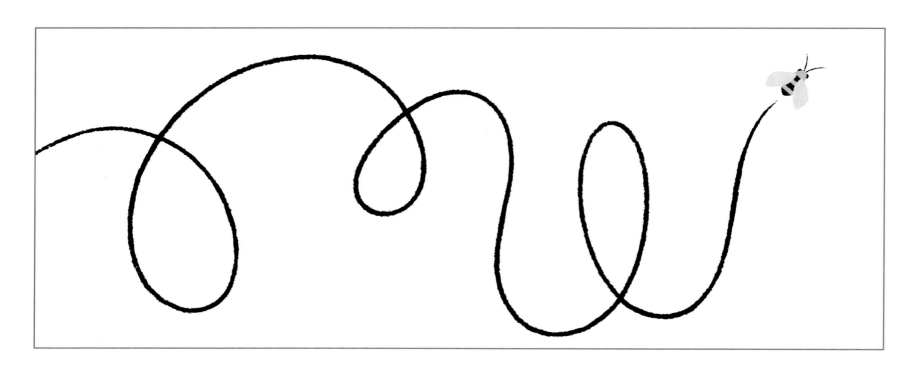

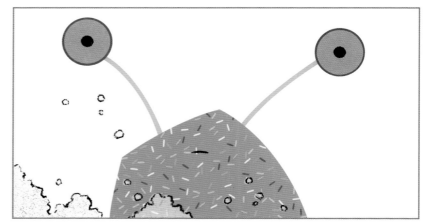

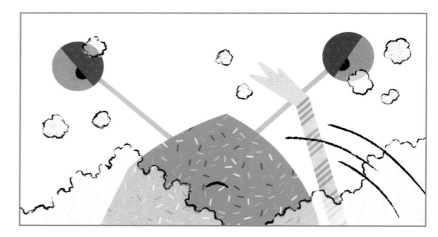

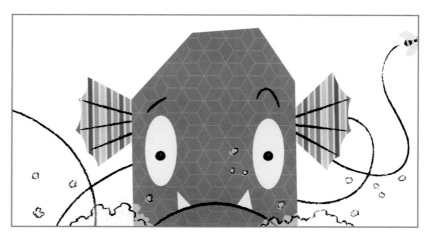

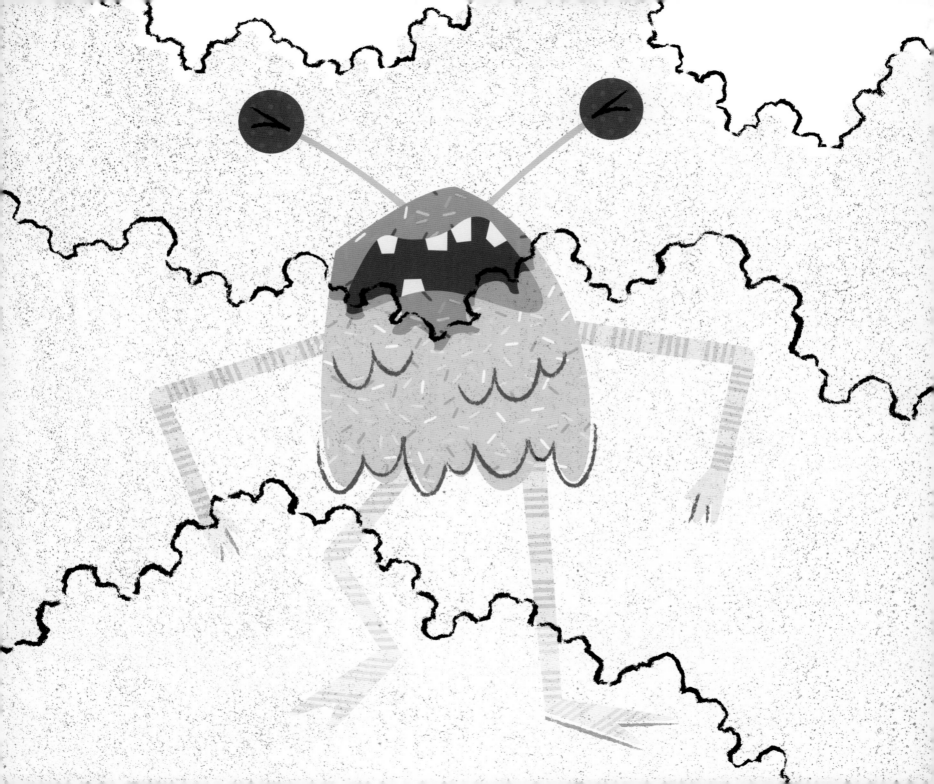

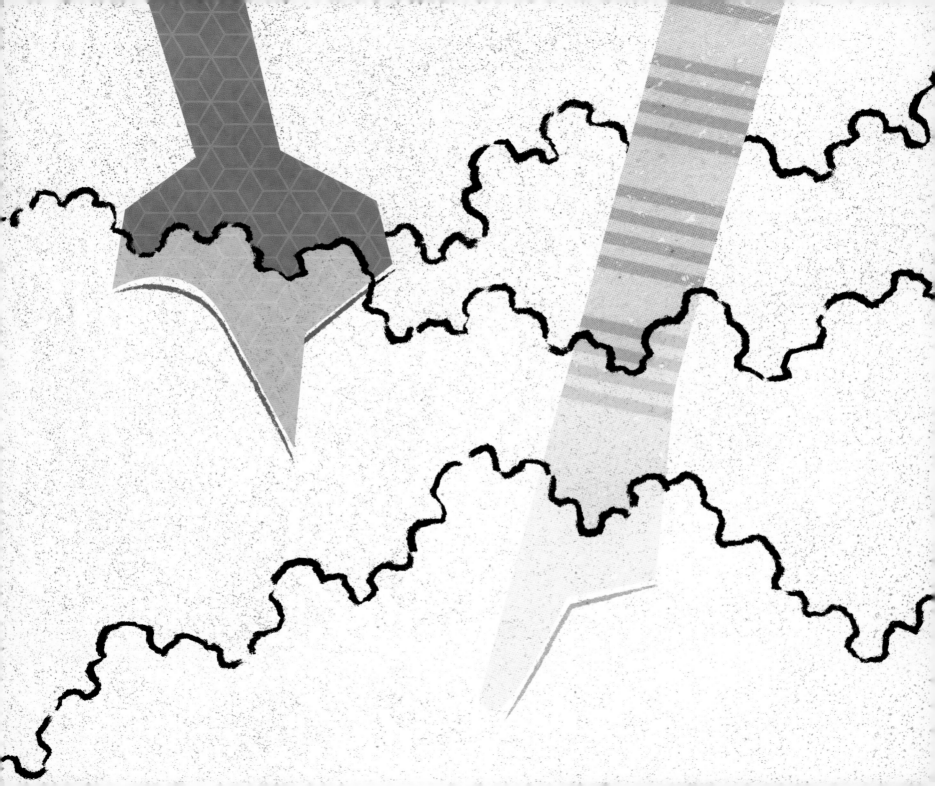

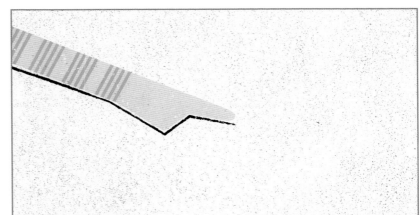
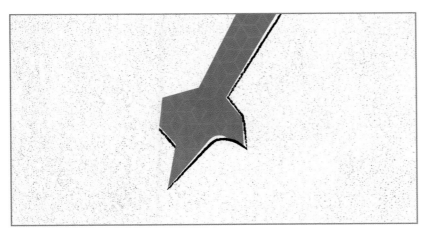
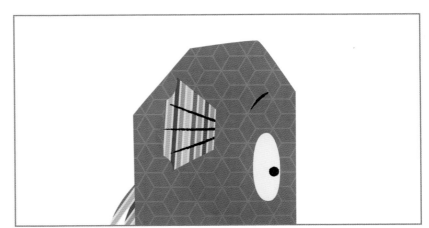
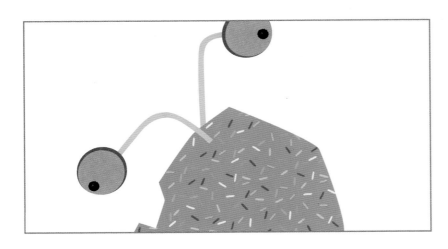
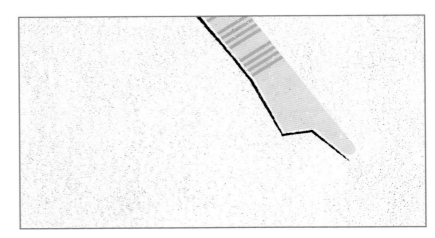